SECURITY
This book belongs to

SECURITY
T.rex Team

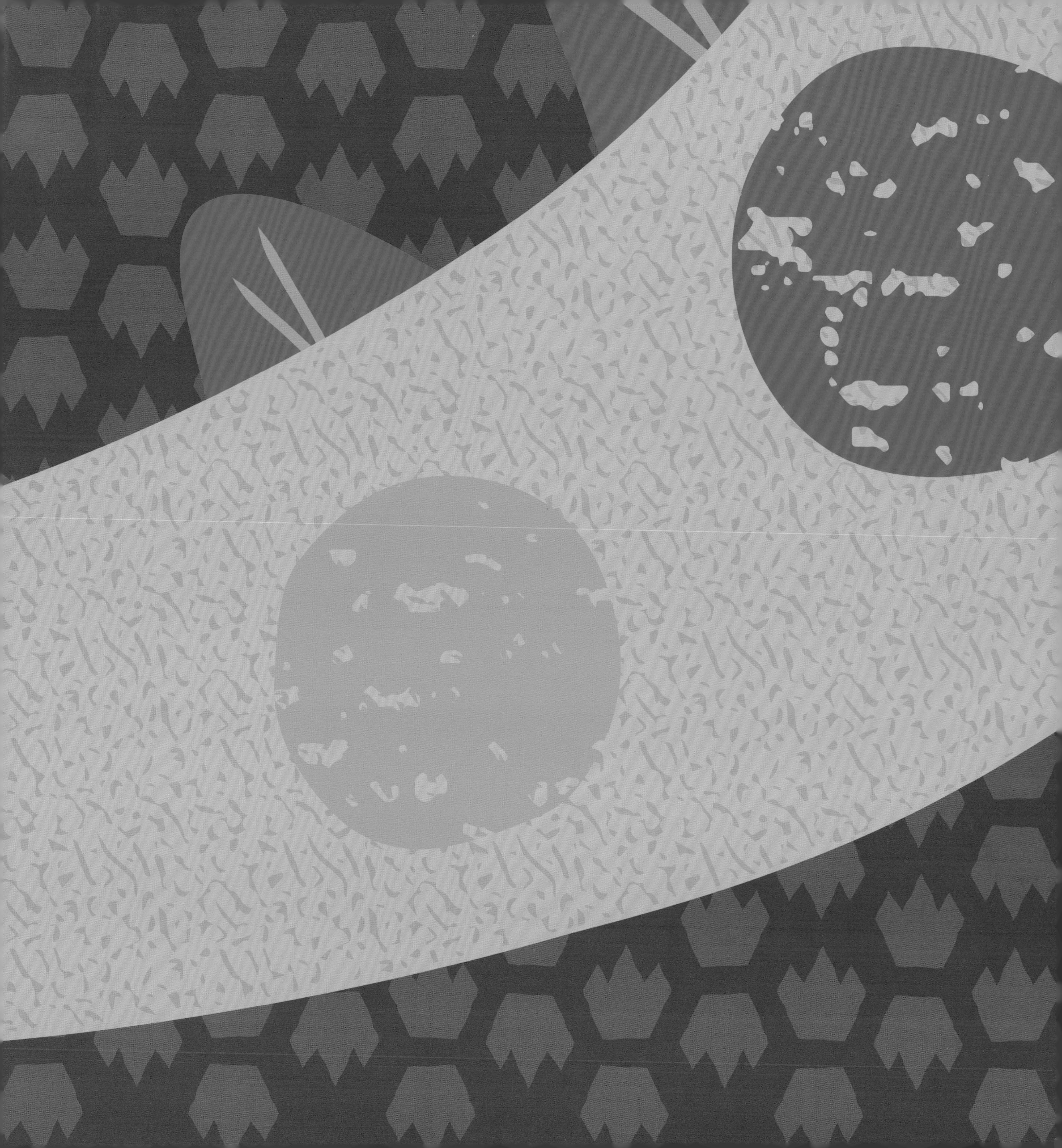

make believe ideas ltd
The Wilderness, Berkhamsted, Hertfordshire, HP4 2AZ, UK.
501 Nelson Place, P.O. Box 141000, Nashville, TN 37214-1000, USA.

www.makebelieveideas.com

Written by Rosie Greening.
Illustrated by Stuart Lynch.

NEVER touch A T.rex

Rosie Greening • Stuart Lynch

make believe ideas

Hey, you!

I know why you're here.

You want to touch the T. rex, don't you?

WELL YOU CAN'T.

My job is to keep the T. rex safe from people like you.

Here's the rule:

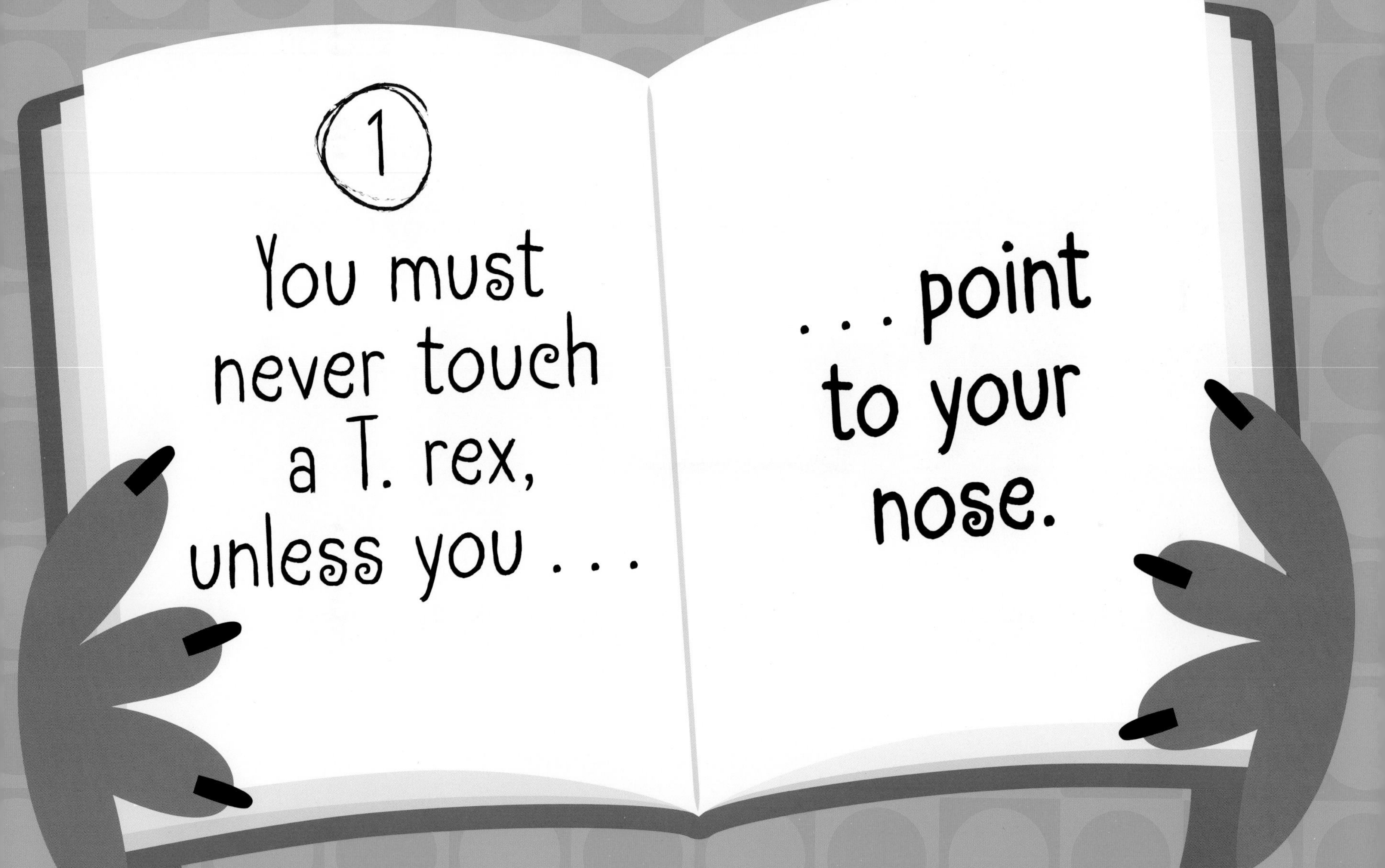

There's no way you can point to your nose. Just you try!

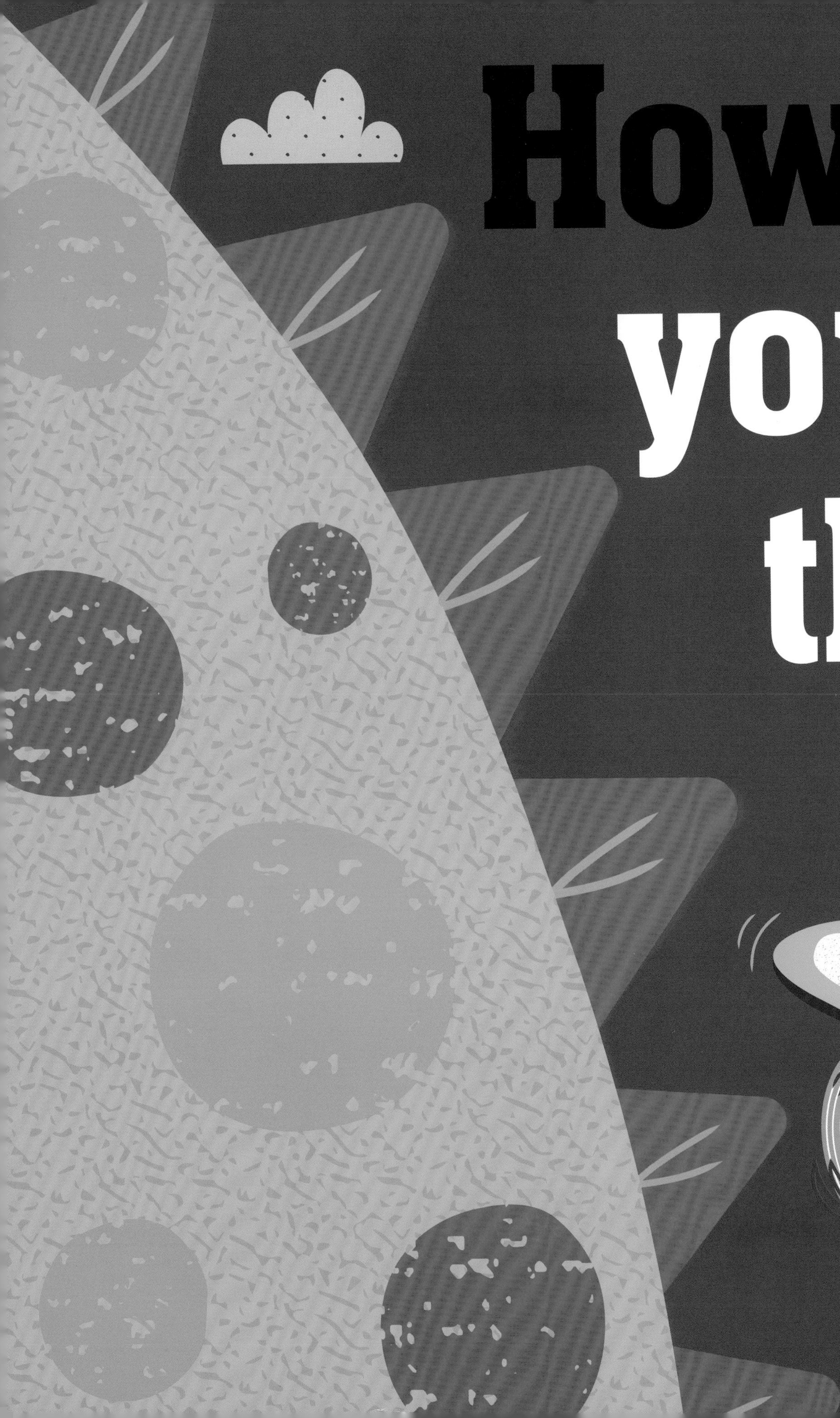

How did you do that?

Okay, this is the **real** rule.

You must **never** touch a **T. rex**,

unless you . . .

. . . **POINT** to your nose

and **TOUCH** your toes!

Ha! Try those if you

think you're so clever.

Okay, **genius.**

The **actual** rule is this:

Never touch a T. rex,

unless you . . .

point to your nose,

touch your toes,

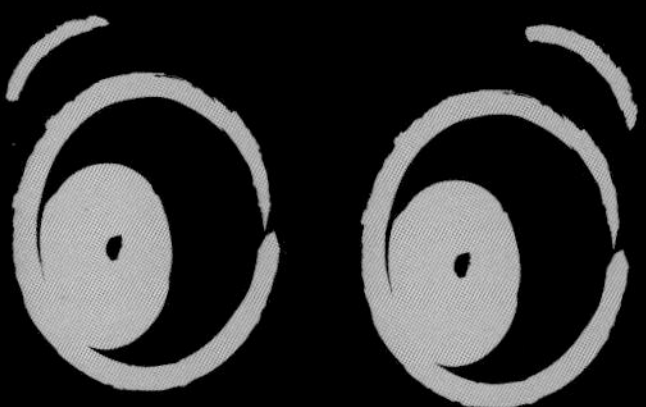

and find a rose.

GOTCHA!

You won't find a rose on this page.

How **are** you **DOING** **this?**

Right. EVEN YOU won't be able to . . .

touch your toes,
find a rose,
and shout,
"Banana!"

Have you done this before?

It's **lucky** I have a plan . . .

You must never touch a T. rex,
unless you . . .

. . . point to your nose,

touch your toes,

find a rose,

Shout, "BANANA!"

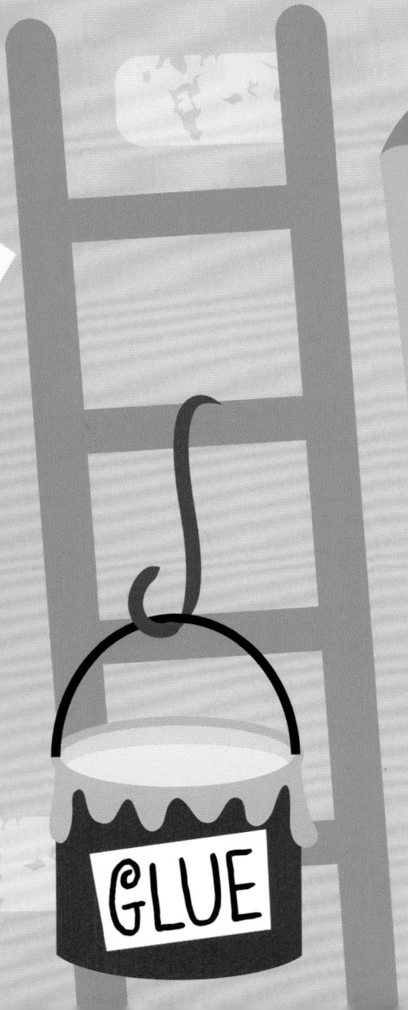

Wave at me,

I COUNT to three,

1 2 3

meow
like a cat,
FLAP
like a
BAT,
SECURITY
T.rex
Team
Raptor
sing HIGH,
then low,
SAAAAAAAY
SOOOMETHIIIIIING
SLOOOOOWWWW...

...ARRRRRR
SECURITY
GLUE

GH!

"HELLO!

Sorry about the guard.

There's really only **one** rule you need to know.

You must **never** touch a T. rex,
unless you . . .

ASK POLITELY.

Go on, **give it a try!**"

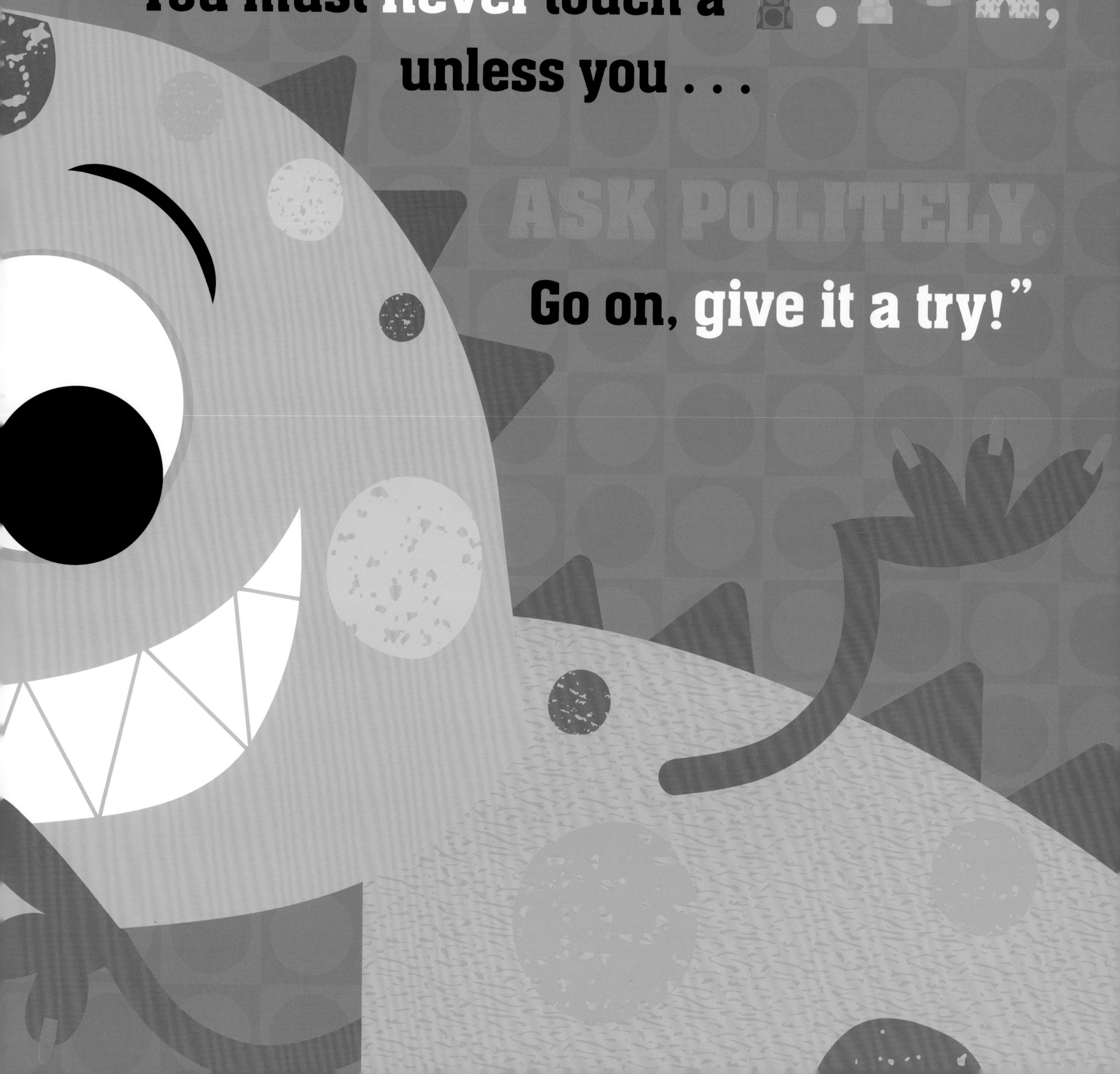

"How **nice** and **polite** you are!

OF COURSE YOU CAN!"

Okay, okay.

You're brighter than I thought.

But I've got one more rule for you:

DON'T CLOSE this book!

SECURITY
T.rex Team
Raptor

SECURITY
GLUE
Raptor